The publishers are grateful for permission to reproduce the following material.

From *Where's Waldo? The Ultimate Fun Book* by Martin Handford. Copyright ©1990 by Martin Handford. By permission of Little, Brown and Company.

From *I Never Saw A Purple Cow* by Emma Chichester Clark. Illustrations and text compilation copyright ©1990 by Emma Chichester Clark. By permission of Little, Brown and Company.

From *Mrs. Goose's Baby* by Charlotte Voake. Copyright ©1989 by Charlotte Voake. By permission of Little, Brown and Company, in association with Joy Street Books.

All text and two illustrations from *Hello, Goodbye* by David Lloyd, illustrated by Louise Voce. Text: Copyright ©1988 by David Lloyd. Ill: Copyright © 1988 by Louise Voce. By permission of Lothrop, Lee & Shepard Books, a division of William Morrow & Company, Inc..

Seven pages of text and six illustrations from *The Big Concrete Lorry* by Shirley Hughes. Text: Copyright © 1989 by Shirley Hughes. Ill: Copyright © 1989 by Shirley Hughes. By permission of Lothrop, Lee & Shepard Books, a division of William Morrow & Company, Inc..

All text and four illustrations from *We Love Them* by Martin Waddell, illustrated by Barbara Firth. Text: Copyright © 1990 by Martin Waddell. Ill: Copyright © 1990 by Barbara Firth. By permission of Lothrop, Lee & Shepard Books, a division of William Morrow & Company, Inc..

All text and five illustrations from *Eat Up, Gemma* by Sarah Hayes, illustrated by Jan Ormerod. Text: Copyright © 1988 by Sarah Hayes. Ill: Copyright © 1988 by Jan Ormerod. By permission of Lothrop, Lee & Shepard Books, a division of William Morrow & Company, Inc.

Excerpts from *Edmond Went Far Away*, text copyright © 1989, 1988 by Martin Bax, illustration copyright © 1988 by Michael Foreman, reprinted by permission of Harcourt Brace Jovanovich, Inc.

Excerpt and illustrations from *Melisande* by E. Nesbit, illustration copyright © 1989 by P.J. Lynch, reprinted by permission of Harcourt Brace Jovanovich, Inc.

From *When The Walrus Comes* by Chris Riddell, Author and Illustrator. Copyright © 1989 by Chris Riddell. Used by permission of Dell Books, a division of Bantam Doubleday Dell Publishing Group, Inc.

Beaky by Jez Alborough. Copyright © 1990 by Jez Alborough. Reprinted by permission of Houghton Mifflin Company. All rights reserved.

The Grumpalump by Sarah Hayes, illustrated by Barbara Firth. Text copyright © 1990 by Sarah Hayes. Illustrations copyright © 1990 by Barbara Firth. Reprinted by permission of Clarion Books, a Houghton Mifflin Company imprint. All rights reserved.

From *Pog*. Copyright © 1989 by Peter Haswell. Reprinted with permission of the publisher, Orchard Books.

Reprinted with permission of Macmillan Publishing Company from *As I Was Going Up and Down and Other Nonsense Rhymes*, illustrated by Nicola Bayley. Illustrations Copyright © 1985 by Nicola Bayley.

Reprinted with permission of Aladdin Books, an imprint of Macmillan Publishing Company from *Tickle, Tickle* by Helen Oxenbury. Copyright © 1987 Helen Oxenbury.

Reprinted with permission of Margaret K. McElderry Books, an imprint of Macmillan Publishing Company from *Sally and the Limpet* by Simon James. Copyright © 1990 Simon James.

If I Could Work by Terence Blacker, Illustrated by Chris Winn. Text copyright ©1988 by Terence Blacker, Illustration Copyright ©1988 by Chris Winn. Reprinted by permission of HarperCollins Publishers.

Duck by David Lloyd, Illustrated by Charlotte Voake. Text Copyright © 1988 by David Lloyd, Illustration Copyright © 1988 by Charlotte Voake. Reprinted by permission of HarperCollins Publishers.

From the book, *A House In Town* by William Mayne and Sarah Fox-Davies copyright © 1987. Used by permission of the publisher, Simon and Schuster, Inc. New York.

From the book, *Little Rabbit Foo Foo* by Michael Rosen and Arthur Robins copyright © 1990. Used by permission of the publisher, Simon and Schuster Books for Young Readers, New York, NY.

From the book, *Jolly Roger* by Colin McNaughton copyright © 1988. Used by permission of the publisher, Simon and Schuster, Inc. New York.

Little Beaver and the Echo by Amy MacDonald, illustrated by Sarah Fox-Davies, text copyright © 1990 by Amy MacDonald, illustrations copyright © 1990 by Sarah Fox-Davies. Reprinted by permission of G. P. Putnam's Sons.

All In One Piece by Jill Murphy, text and illustrations copyright © 1987 by Jill Murphy. Reprinted by permission of G.P. Putnam's Sons.

From *I Like Books* by Anthony Browne. Copyright © 1988 Anthony Browne. Reprinted with permission of the publisher, Alfred A. Knopf, Inc.

First U.S. edition 1992. First published in Great Britain in 1992 by Walker Books Ltd., London. ISBN 1-56402-113-0

Library of Congress Catalog Card Number 91-71859. Library of Congress Cataloging-in-Publication Data is available.

10 9 8 7 6 5 4 3 2 1

Printed in Hong Kong

CANDLEWICK PRESS, 2067 MASSACHUSETTS AVENUE, CAMBRIDGE, MASSACHUSETTS 02140

BIG BEAR'S TREASURY

A Children's Anthology

CANDLEWICK PRESS
CAMBRIDGE, MASSACHUSETTS

CONTENTS

This book is a second collection of Big Bear's favorite stories and pictures. In Volume One, you found classics like *Five Minutes' Peace* by Jill Murphy, and *Tom and Pippo Read a Story* by Helen Oxenbury. In Volume Two, you'll find more great stories and poems to read. In choosing a selection, you might want to just leaf through the book until something catches your eye. It might be a special picture or the title of a story or poem. Or it might be something that reflects the mood you are in at the moment. Perhaps you'd like a bedtime story, or perhaps you are feeling silly and want a good laugh...

With thirty-five selections to choose from, there are lots and lots of treasures waiting, new stories and artwork to be discovered and enjoyed for the very first time. Once you know the selections, you can turn to the contents page again and again to find your favorites. Of course if you're older, you can read your favorites yourself or read them out loud to your younger sisters and brothers. Good children's poems and stories stand up to the test of time—they're the ones you and your parents will want to read over and over again.

Goodbye!

I LIKE BOOKS

by Anthony Browne

I like books.
Funny books
and scary books.
Fairy tales
and nursery
rhymes.
Comic books
and coloring books.
Fat books
and thin books.
Books about
dinosaurs,
and books about
monsters.
Counting books
and alphabet books.

8

Books about space,
and books
about pirates.

Song books
and strange books.

Yes,
I really
do like
books.

9

WHEN THE WALRUS COMES
by Chris Riddell

It's always fun when the walrus comes to visit. It's fun when we do things and fun when we don't. One day we packed our bags and set sail in the *Phoebe McBean*. We sailed up and down and round and round until we came to an island where monkeys live. The monkeys helped us unpack and they helped us eat our sandwiches. They showed us all the things that monkeys like to do, like climbing trees and swinging on vines and hanging upside down.

And we showed them what we like to do, like standing on our heads and doing cartwheels and making funny faces. Then the walrus played to us on the curly-wurly Eudophone, and we had fun being noisy. And we had fun being quiet when the moon and stars came out. That's how it is—it's always fun when the walrus comes to visit.

11

Rosie's Babies

by
**Martin
Waddell**

illustrated by
**Penny
Dale**

Mom was putting
the baby to bed and
Rosie said,
"I have two babies
and you only
have one."
"Two, including you,"
said Mom.
"I'm not a baby,
I'm four years old,"
said Rosie.
"Tell me about
your babies,"
Mom said.

And Rosie said,
"My babies live in a
bird's nest and they
are almost as big as
me. They go outside
all by themselves and
sometimes they make
me mad!"
"Do they?" said Mom.
"Yes. When they
do silly things!"
said Rosie.
"What silly things do
they do?" asked Mom.

And Rosie said,
"My babies climbed
a big mountain. That
was silly, because
they couldn't get
down. They jumped,
and they bumped
on their bottoms!"
"Silly babies,"
said Mom.
"Did they hurt
themselves?"

And Rosie said,
"One of my babies
hurt her knee.
I bandaged it up and
she cried and I said,
'It's o.k.,' because I'm
nice."
"I'm sure you are," said
Mom. "What else do
your babies do?"

And Rosie said,
"My babies drive cars
that are real, and
trucks and boats.
My babies are very
good drivers."
"What do your babies
like doing the most?"
asked Mom.

And Rosie said,
"My babies like swings
and rocking chairs
and dinosaurs. They
go to the park when
it's dark and there are
no moms and dads
who can see, only
me!"
"Oh my!" said Mom.
"Aren't they scared?"

And Rosie said,
"My babies are scared
of the big dogs,
but I'm not. I go
GRRRRRRRRRRRRRR!
and frighten the big
dogs away."
"They are not
very scared then?"
said Mom.
"My babies know
I will take care of
them," said Rosie.

"I'm their mom."
"How do you take care
of them?"
Mom asked.

And Rosie said,
"I make their snacks
and I tell them
stories and I take
them for walks and
I talk to them and
I tell them that I
love them."

"That's a good way
to take care of
babies!" said Mom.
"Do you make
them nice things
to eat, like pies?"

And Rosie said,
"My babies make
their own pies, but
they never eat them."
"What do they eat?"
asked Mom.

And Rosie thought and thought and thought, and then Rosie said,

"My babies went to bed."

"Just like this one," said Mom.

"I don't want to talk about my babies anymore because they are asleep," said Rosie.

"I don't want them to wake up, or they'll cry."

"We could talk very softly," said Mom.

"Yes," said Rosie.

"What will we talk about?" asked Mom.

And Rosie said,

"ME!"

And Rosie said, "My babies eat apples and apples and apples all the time. And grapes and pears but they don't like the seeds."

"Most babies don't," said Mom.

"Are you going to tell me more about your babies?"

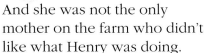

THE WHISTLING PIGLET

by Dick King-Smith
illustrated by Norman Johnson

"Who's that whistling?" said Mompig. "What an awful noise!"

"It's Henry," said nine of her ten spotted piglets.

Henry, the tenth piglet, didn't say anything because he was busy whistling. He pursed up his little mouth and whistled like a blackbird.

"And it's not an awful noise!" cried his brothers and sisters. "It's great! It's catchy! It makes your feet itch!" and they all began to dance around Henry.

"How embarrassing!" grunted Mompig. "To think that I am the mother of the world's first whistling piglet!"

And she was not the only mother on the farm who didn't like what Henry was doing.

"Who's that whistling?" mooed the cows. "What a horrible sound!"

"Who's that whistling?" bleated the sheep. "What a dreadful din!"

"Who's that whistling?" cackled the hens. "What a terrible racket!"

But their young ones did not agree. "It's not a horrible sound!" cried the calves and, "It's not a dreadful din!" cried the lambs and, "It's not a terrible racket!" cried the baby chicks. And they all said, "It's great! It's catchy! It makes your feet itch!" and they all began to dance.

As well as being great and catchy and making their feet itch, there was one particular tune that Henry sometimes whistled that made all the young animals feel that they would run after him, wherever he went. It was the tune of the song whose words go like this:

Come follow, follow, follow,
Follow, follow, follow me.
Whither shall I follow,
follow, follow,
Whither shall I follow,
follow thee?
To the greenwood,
to the greenwood,
To the greenwood,
greenwood tree.

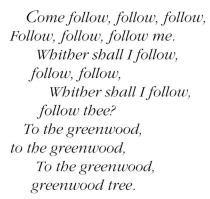

16

Every time Henry whistled that tune, the calves would break out of their pens; and the lambs would jump out of their fields; and the chicks would flutter out of their runs; and all would run to follow Henry. How angry the farmer was!

Almost every day he had to catch all the young animals and put them back where they belonged.

"And all because of that whistling piglet!" he said to his wife and his little daughter. "What a horrible hullabaloo!"

"It is!" said his wife.

"It's not!" said his little daughter. "It's great! It's catchy! It makes your feet itch!"

"They won't itch much longer," said the farmer. "I'm sending him to market next Friday."

Next Friday a truck came to the farm and pulled up outside Mompig's sty.

"What's that for, Mompig?" asked nine of her ten spotted piglets. Henry didn't ask because he was too busy whistling.

"It's to take you to market."

"What happens there?" they asked.

"Someone will buy you and fatten you up," said Mompig. Henry stopped whistling.

"What for?" he said.

"Never mind," said Mompig. "Don't worry about that. Just get in the truck."

But Henry did worry. He did not think that this little piggy wanted to go to market. He waited until the sty door was opened and then he began to whistle the tune of the song whose words go like this:

Come follow, follow, follow,
Follow, follow, follow me.
Whither shall I follow,
follow, follow,
Whither shall I follow,
follow thee?
To the greenwood,
to the greenwood,
To the greenwood,
greenwood tree.

And he ran as fast as he could, whistling as loud as he could, past the truck and across the farmyard and out into the fields and away to the greenwood. And after him ran his nine brothers and sisters. And after them the calves came galloping, and the lambs came gamboling, and the chicks came fluttering…all following

the sound of that one particular tune that made them feel that wherever the whistling piglet went, there they would go too.

What a business it was for the farmer and his men to catch them all again! But calves and lambs are not really happy in the depths of a greenwood (there's not enough grass), nor are chicks (there are too many foxes), and at last they caught them all and took them back to the farm. The piglets, though, were a different matter, for pigs love woods that are full of acorns and beechnuts and mushrooms and other wonderful things to eat. So it took the farmer and his men a long time to catch nine of Mompig's ten spotted children. They never caught the tenth one. They searched the greenwood for weeks and weeks, but found nothing. All they heard—now and then —was the sound of someone whistling.

A Zoo in

Mom and I went to
the zoo.
I said, "Can I have a zoo
in our house?"
"Certainly not," said Mom.

But…

…on Monday a giraffe
was eating in
the kitchen.

On Tuesday
a hippopotamus was
splashing in the tub.

On Wednesday a monkey
was swinging in the hall.

On Thursday
a crocodile was washing
in the garden.

Our House

by Heather Eyles
illustrated by Andy Cooke

On Friday a lion was sleeping in the living room.

On Saturday all the animals came and we had a party.

On Sunday Mom sent them all back to the zoo.

"Phew," said Mom.

But...

...she forgot the gorilla.

19

An excerpt from
Hans Christian
Andersen's

THE

SNOW QUEEN

translated by Naomi Lewis
illustrated by
Angela Barrett

Out in the square the boldest boys would often tie their sleds to farmers' carts, and be pulled along for quite a ride. It was a great deal of fun. This time, while their games were in full swing, a very large sled arrived; it was painted white all over, and in it sat a figure muffled up in a white fur cloak and wearing a white fur hat. This sled drove twice round the square, but moving quickly, Kay managed to tie his own sled behind it, and a swift ride began. The big sled went faster and faster, then turned off into the next street. The driver looked around and nodded to Kay in the friendliest way, just as if they had always known each other. Every time that Kay thought of untying his sled, the driver would turn and nod to him again, so he kept still. On they drove, straight out of the city gates. And now the snow began to fall so thick and fast that the little boy couldn't even see his hand in front of him as they rushed along. At last he did manage to untie the rope but it was of no use; his little sled still clung to the big one, and they sped along like the wind. He cried out at the top of his voice, but no one heard him; the snow fell, and the sled raced on. From time to time it seemed to jump, as if they were going over dikes and hedges. Terror seized him, he tried to say the Lord's Prayer, but all he could remember was the multiplication tables.

The snowflakes grew bigger and bigger until at last they looked like great white birds. All at once they swerved to one side; the sled came to a halt and the driver stood up. The white fur cloak and cap were all of snow and the driver—ah, she was a lady, tall and slender, dazzlingly white! She was the Snow Queen herself.

"We've come far and fast," she said. "But you must be frozen. Crawl under my bearskin cloak." She put him beside her in the sled and wrapped the cloak around him; he felt as if he were sinking into a snowdrift. "Are you still cold?" she asked, and she kissed him on the forehead. Ah-h-h! Her kiss was colder than ice; it went straight to his heart, which was already halfway to being a lump of ice. He felt as if he were dying, but only for a moment. Then he felt perfectly well, and no longer noticed the cold.

"My sled! Don't forget my sled!" That was the first thought that came to him. So it was tied to one of the big white birds, which flew along with the little sled at its back. The Snow Queen kissed Kay once again, and after that he had no memory of Gerda and the grandmother, nor of anyone at home.

"Now I must give you no more kisses," said the Snow Queen, "or you will be kissed to death."

Kay looked at her. She was so beautiful; he could not imagine a wiser, lovelier face. She no longer seemed to him to be made of ice, as she once had when she came to the attic window and waved to him. Now in his eyes she was perfect, and he felt no fear. He told her that he could do mental arithmetic and fractions, too; that he knew the square miles of all the principal countries, and their populations. As he talked she smiled at him, until he began to think that what he knew was, after all, not quite so much. And he looked up into the vast expanse of the sky as they rose up high, and she flew with him over the dark clouds, while the storm-wind whistled and raved, making him think of ballads of olden time. Over forest and lake they flew, over sea and land. Beneath them screamed the icy blast; the wolves howled, the snow glittered, the black crows soared across the plains, cawing as they went. But high over all shone the great clear silver moon, and Kay gazed up at it all through the long, long winter night. During the day he slept at the Snow Queen's feet.

Little Beaver and the Echo

by Amy MacDonald
illustrated by Sarah Fox-Davies

Little Beaver lived all alone by the edge of a big pond. He didn't have any brothers. He didn't have any sisters.

Worst of all, he didn't have any friends. One day, sitting by the side of the pond, he began to cry. He cried out loud. Then he cried out louder.

Suddenly, he heard something very strange. On the other side of the pond, someone else was crying too. Little Beaver stopped crying and listened. The other crying stopped. Little Beaver was alone again.

"Booo hooo," he said.

"Booo hooo," said the voice from across the pond.

"Huh-huh-waaah!" said Little Beaver.

"Huh-huh-waaah!" said the voice from across the pond.

Little Beaver stopped crying.

"Hello!" he called.

"Hello!" said the voice from across the pond.

"Why are you crying?" asked Little Beaver.

"Why are you crying?" asked the voice from across the pond.

Little Beaver thought for a moment.

"I'm lonely," he said. "I need a friend."

"I'm lonely," said the voice from across the pond. "I need a friend."

Little Beaver couldn't believe it. On the other side of the pond lived somebody else who was sad and needed a friend.

He got right into his boat and set off to find him.

It was a big pond. He paddled and paddled. Then he saw a young duck, swimming in circles all by himself.

"I'm looking for someone who needs a friend," said Little Beaver.

"Was it you who was crying?"

"I do need a friend," said the duck.

"But it wasn't me who was crying."

"I'll be your friend," said Little Beaver. "Come with me."

So the duck jumped into the boat. They paddled and paddled. Then they saw a young otter, sliding up and down the bank all by himself.

"We're looking for someone who
   needs a friend," said Little Beaver.
"Was it you who was crying?"
"I do need a friend," said
   the otter. "But it
   wasn't me who
   was crying."
"We'll be your friends," said
   Little Beaver and the duck.
"Come with us."
   So the otter jumped into the boat.
   They paddled and paddled. Then
   they saw a young turtle, sunning
   himself all alone on a rock.
"We're looking for someone who
   needs a friend," said Little Beaver.
"Was it you who was crying?"
"I do need a friend," said the turtle.
"But it wasn't me who was crying."
"We'll be your friends," said Little
   Beaver and the duck and the otter.
"Come with us."
   So the turtle jumped into the boat,
   and they paddled and paddled until
   they came to the end of the pond.

Here lived a wise old beaver in a
   mud house, all alone. Little Beaver
   told him how they had paddled all
   around the pond to find out who
   was crying.
"It wasn't the duck," Little Beaver said.
"It wasn't the otter. And it wasn't
   the turtle. Who was it?"
"It was the Echo," said the wise
   old beaver.
"Where does he live?" asked Little
   Beaver.
"On the other side of the pond,"
   said the wise old beaver. "No matter
   where you are, the Echo is always
   across the pond from you."
"Why is he crying?" said Little Beaver.

24

"When you are sad, the Echo
is sad," said the wise old beaver.
"When you are happy, the Echo
is happy too."
"But how can I find him and be his
friend?" asked Little Beaver. "He
doesn't have any friends, and
neither do I."
"Except for me," said the duck.
"And me," said the otter.
"And me," said the turtle.
Little Beaver looked surprised.
"Yes," he said, "I have lots of friends
now!" And he was so happy that he
said it again, very loudly: "I have lots
of friends now!"

From across the
pond, a voice
answered him:
"I have lots of
friends now!"
"You see?"
said the wise
old beaver. "When
you're happy, the Echo is
happy. When you have friends, he
has friends too."
"Hooray!" shouted Little Beaver and
the duck and the otter and the turtle,
all together. And the Echo shouted
back to them:
"Hooray!"

25

If I could work
instead of play,

I'd get up early
every day.

I'd drive a bus
and shout,
"Fares, please!"

I'd rescue
cats from
the tops of trees.

I'd be an inventor
and make lots
of toys.

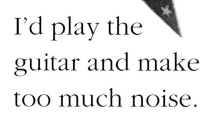

I'd play the
guitar and make
too much noise.

I'd be the world's
favorite TV star.

I'd be a doctor
and make
children say,
"Aaaah."

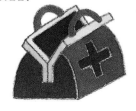

I'd open a shop
with candy on
the shelf.

When no one
was looking I'd
eat them
myself.

by Terence Blacker
illustrated by Chris Winn

I'd smile at people as they drove past. I'd stop them if they went too fast.

I'd be an incredibly funny clown. I'd make people laugh when my pants fell down.

I'd be the first child to go to the moon. I'd tell my parents I'd be back soon. And I'd fly back home at the end of the day—

I'd really much rather work than play.

27

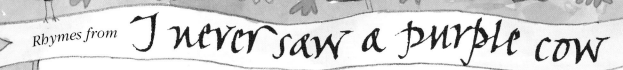

I never saw a purple cow

THERE WAS A YOUNG MAIDEN

There was a young maiden called Maggie
Whose dog was hairy and shaggy;
The front end of him was vicious and grim
But the tail end was friendly and waggy.

THERE WAS A LITTLE DOG

There was a little dog and he had a tail
And he used to wag, wag, wag it!
But when he was sad, because he'd been bad,
On the ground he would drag, drag, drag it!

Illustrated by EMMA Chichester Clark

I'VE GOT A DOG

I've got a dog as thin as a rail,
He's got fleas all over his tail;
Every time his tail goes *flop*,
The fleas on the bottom all hop to the top.

DING, DONG, DARROW

Ding, dong, darrow,
The cat and the sparrow;
The little dog has burnt his tail,
And he shall be whipped tomorrow.

An excerpt from # JOLLY

"My mom," said Roger to the pirates, who were all ears (well, maybe not *all* ears as some seemed to be missing one or the other), "my mom is the cleanest, neatest person in the whole world! And she wants me to be just like her.

Every day it's the same—up before dawn, make the bed, straighten my room, get washed (here there were cries of horror from the pirates), comb my hair ('WHAT'S A COMB?'), eat my breakfast, wash the dishes, bake the bread, brush my teeth (*Gasp*!), churn the butter, scrub the floors, iron the clothes, clean the pigsty, wash the cow, polish the goat, shampoo the chicken, whitewash the coal—on and on and on!"

Well, it was almost true, thought Roger, crossing his fingers behind his back.

"Poor wee scab!" growled the captain.

30

ROGER

by Colin McNaughton

"A livin' 'ell! Oooh-aargh! It ain't right fer a lad t'be brought up s'clean! By the curse of Eric the Yobbo! 'T ain't natural like! No, kids should be smelly and 'orrible! 'Tis the only chance they gits afore they grows up inter people! The only chance that be, oooh-aargh, unless they become pirates, ha-har! Then they can be dirty, smelly, lazy, an' 'orrible all their lives! Ya-har! Curse y'all! Oooh-aargh! Ya-har!"

This fine speech by the captain was much appreciated by his crew, who cheered him and shouted things like "Yeah, that's why I joined up!" and "I'll drink t'that!" and "Down wi' soap!"

"That there mother o' yourn needs t'be taught a lesson! And we be just the chappies to be a-doin' it!" growled Abdul.

"What sez 'ee, me shoal o' sharks, eh? Should we go an' shiver 'er timbers?"

The crew replied with cries of "Aye!" and "Sounds o.k. to me." And so the pirates went, as pirates do, a-cursing and a-swearing, a-hooting and a-hollering, enough to give a boy a very bad headache.

31

Duck

by David Lloyd

illustrations by Charlotte Voake

 There was a time, long ago, when Tim called all animals duck.
"Duck," Tim said.
"Horse," said Granny.
"Duck," Tim said.
"Sheep," said Granny.
"Duck," Tim said.
"Chicken," said Granny.
 So Granny took Tim to the pond.
"Duck," she said.
Tim looked and looked.
"Duck," he said.
Granny kissed him.

A little later
Tim saw a tractor.
"Truck," he said.
A little later
Tim saw a bus.
"Truck," he said.
A little later
Tim saw an old car.
"Truck," he said.
So Granny showed Tim a truck.
"Truck," she said.
Tim looked and looked.
"Truck," he said.
Granny kissed him.

32

For some time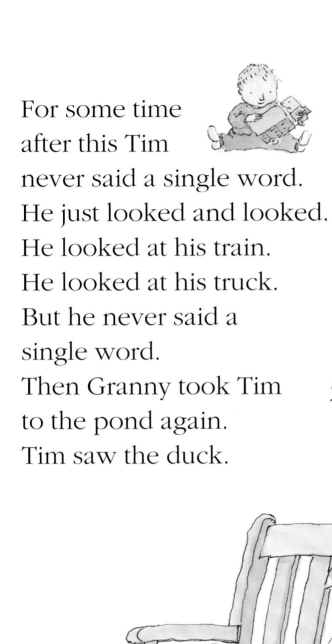
after this Tim
never said a single word.
He just looked and looked.
He looked at his train.
He looked at his truck.
But he never said a
single word.
Then Granny took Tim
to the pond again.
Tim saw the duck.

He looked and looked.
The duck said, "Quack!"
"Duck," Tim said.
"Duck," Granny said.
Granny kissed Tim.
Tim kissed Granny.

All in One Piece

by Jill Murphy

Mr. Large was getting ready for work. "Don't forget the office dinner-dance tonight, dear," he said.

"Of course I won't," said Mrs. Large. "I've been thinking about it all year."

"Are children allowed at the dinner-dance?" asked Lester.

"No," said Mrs. Large. "It'll be too late for children."

"What about the baby?" asked Luke.

"Granny is coming to take care of everyone," said Mrs. Large, "so there's no need to worry." Granny arrived at dinner time. The children were already washed up and in their pajamas. Granny gave them some painting to do while she straightened up and Mr. and Mrs. Large went upstairs to get ready. Luke sneaked into the bathroom while Mr. Large was shaving.

"Will I have to shave when I grow up?" he asked, patting foam onto his trunk.

"Go away," said Mr. Large. "I don't want you ruining my best slacks!"

The baby crept into the bedroom where Mrs. Large was putting on her make-up. Mrs. Large didn't notice until it was too late.

"Look!" said the baby.

"Pretty!"

"Don't move," said Mrs. Large. "Don't touch *anything!*"

Outside on the landing, things were even worse. Laura was clopping around in her mother's best shoes and necklace, and Lester and Luke were seeing how many toys they could cram into their mother's new tights.

"Downstairs right *now!*" bellowed Mrs. Large. "Can't I have just one night in the whole year to myself? One night when I am not covered in jam and poster-paint? One night when I can put on my new dress and walk through the front door all in one piece?"

The children went downstairs to Granny. Mr. Large followed soon after, very sharp in his best suit. At last, Mrs. Large appeared in the doorway.

"How do I look?" she asked.

"Pretty, Mommy!" gasped the children.

"What a knock-out!" said Mr. Large.

"You look like a movie star, dear," said Granny.

34

"Hands off!" said Mrs. Large to the paint-covered children.

Mr. and Mrs. Large got ready to leave.

"Goodbye, everyone," they said. "Be good now."

The baby began to cry.

"Just go," said Granny, picking her up. "She'll stop as soon as you're gone. Have a lovely time."

"We've escaped," said Mr. Large with a smile, closing the front door behind them. "All in one piece," said Mrs. Large, "and not a smear of paint between us."

"Actually," said Mr. Large gallantly, "you'd look wonderful to me, even if you were *covered* in paint."

Which was perfectly true… and just as well, actually!

35

Squelch, squelch, in the mud,

Splish, splash, scrub-a-dub,

Tickle, Tickle

by Helen Oxenbury

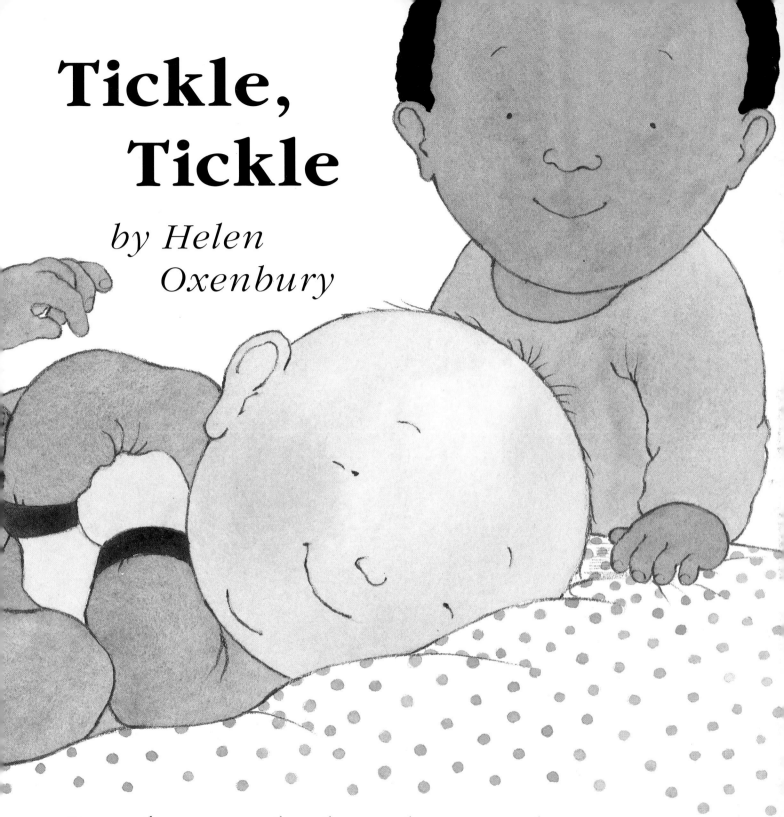

Gently, gently, brush your hair,

Tickle, tickle, under there.

An extract from

Melisande

by E. Nesbit

illustrated by P.J. Lynch

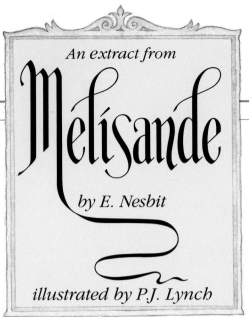

Princess Melisande went on growing. By dinner time she was so large that she had to have her dinner brought out into the garden because she was too large to get indoors. But she was too unhappy to be able to eat anything. And she cried so much that there was quite a pool in the garden, and several pages were almost drowned. So she remembered her *Alice in Wonderland* and stopped crying at once.

But she did not stop growing. She grew bigger and bigger and bigger, until she had to go outside the palace gardens and sit on the common, and even that was too small to hold her comfortably, for every hour she grew twice as much as she had the hour before. And nobody knew what to do, nor where the Princess was to sleep. Fortunately, her clothes had grown with her, or she would have been very cold indeed, and now she sat on the common in her green gown embroidered with gold, looking like a large hill covered with gorse in flower.

You cannot possibly imagine how large the Princess was growing. Her mother stood wringing her hands on the castle tower, and Prince

Florizel looked on broken-hearted, his Princess snatched from his arms and turned into a lady as big as a mountain.

The King did not weep or look on. He sat down at once and wrote to his fairy godmother, asking her advice. He sent a weasel with the letter, and by return of weasel he got his own letter back again, marked "Gone away. Left no address."

It was now, when the Kingdom was plunged into gloom, that a neighboring King took it into his head to send an invading army against the island where Melisande lived. They came in ships and they landed in great numbers, and Melisande looking down from her height saw alien soldiers marching on the sacred soil of her country.

"I don't mind so much now," said she, "if I can really be of some use this size."

And she picked up the army of the enemy in handfuls and double handfuls, and put them back into their ships, and gave a little flip to each transport ship with her finger

38

and thumb, which sent the ships off so fast that they never stopped until they reached their own country, and when they arrived there the whole army to a man said it would rather be court-martialed a hundred times over than go near the place again.

Meanwhile, Melisande, sitting on the highest hill on the island, felt the land trembling and shivering under her giant feet.

"I do believe I'm getting too heavy," she said, and jumped off the island into the sea, which was just up to her ankles. Just then a great fleet of warships and gunboats and torpedo boats came in sight, on their way to attack the island.

Melisande could easily have sunk them all with one kick, but she did not like to do this because it might have drowned the sailors, and besides, it might have swamped the island.

So she simply stooped and picked the island as you would pick a mushroom—for, of course, all islands are supported by a stalk underneath—and carried it away to another part of the world. So when the warships got to where the island was marked on the map they found nothing but sea, and a very rough sea it was, because the Princess had churned it all up with her ankles as she walked away through it with the island.

When Melisande reached a suitable place, very sunny and warm, and with no sharks in the water, she set down the island; and the people made it fast with anchors, and then everyone went to bed, thanking the kind fate that had sent them so great a Princess to help them in their need, and calling her the savior of her country and the bulwark of the nation.

We Love Them

by Martin Waddell
illustrated by Barbara Firth

It lay with Ben. Ben licked it. Becky said that Ben thought it was a little dog, and the rabbit thought Ben was a big rabbit; they didn't know they'd gotten it mixed up. Becky said we wouldn't tell them.

We called our rabbit Zoe. She stayed with Ben. She played with Ben.

We loved them.

Zoe wasn't little for very long. She got big... and bigger... and bigger still, but not as big as Ben.

But Ben was old... and one day Ben died. We were sad and Zoe was sad. She wouldn't eat her lettuce. She sat and sat.

In all the white fields there was one rabbit. It was lost. It was small. It lay in the snow.

Our dog Ben found it. Ben barked. We picked it up and took it home. Becky thought it would die, but it didn't.

There was no Ben for our rabbit, until one day… in the pale hay, there was a puppy.

We took it home. It lay down with Zoe. Becky said our puppy thought Zoe was a dog, and Zoe thought our puppy

was a rabbit; they didn't know they'd gotten it mixed up. Becky said we wouldn't tell them.

The puppy stayed. The puppy played. We loved him, just like we loved Ben.

We called our puppy Little Ben. But Little Ben got big… and bigger… and bigger

still. He got bigger than our rabbit but not as big as old Ben.

Zoe still thinks Little Ben is a rabbit, and Becky says that Zoe doesn't mind.

Becky says that Zoe likes big rabbits.

Zoe and little Ben play with us in the green fields. They are our dog and our rabbit. We love them.

An excerpt from

What-a-Mess

Goes on Television

by Frank Muir   illustrated by Joseph Wright

The story of What-a-Mess's extremely successful but brief (three and a half minutes) television career began with the birthday party he gave for the cat-next-door. What-a-Mess had been shooed out of the house because a visitor was coming, so he held the party in the garden, in his new Savoy-Ritz By-Invitation-Only No-Grown-Ups Luxury Conference and Banqueting Center, which was an old dresser standing in the ditch with its doors missing. The shelves were narrow, so space was limited and the party had to be held on three floors. All his friends were there. What-a-Mess gave the cat-next-door the top floor all to herself (so that there would be no spitting or clawing) and she lay in state on her shelf, purring and blinking and polishing her left ear. The middle floor was a tight squeeze; the Archbishop of Canterbury (now a medium-sized mongrel puppy and growing) had to share it with the hedgehog, Cynthia, and both were fed up when What-a-Mess took the whole ground floor. But the puppy pointed out that he, too, was sharing. He had to make room for his new friend, Ryvita, the ladybug. (He had figured out, all by himself, that the ladybug must be a lady or it would have been called a gentlemanbug, so he christened her Ryvita. He wasn't sure that Ryvita was a regular girl's name, but he thought it was so pretty that it *should* be, even if it wasn't.)

The cat-next-door's birthday party began with a magnificent feast that What-a-Mess had prepared: cheese rinds, the paper from a half pound of butter, an old piece of leather, a soft lump of unidentified substance found in the compost heap that might have been either a failed Coffee Fudge Angel Cake or a rotting boot, a plastic carton with traces of cream still in it, half a fish, walnuts, some envelopes with plenty of glue still on them, and a large piece of coal. The puppy did not know what ladybugs ate, so he tempted Ryvita with a chocolate drop he was saving for himself. The ladybug flew around it, delicately landed on it as if it were a helicopter pad, folded her wings, and went to sleep. After they ate, the animals chased one another at top speed through the flower beds to settle the food in their stomachs. Then they sat on the grass around What-a-Mess while he told them an exciting story. It was one of the true stories his mother had told him about his famous ancestor, Sheik Hassan of Kabul, Personal Snow-Leopard Hunter to His Majesty King Achmad XXXIV.

WHEN DAD CUTS DOWN THE CHESTNUT TREE

When Dad cuts down the chestnut
  tree,
He'll make such things for you and
  me…
A rocking horse to ride all day,
A fort where all my soldiers stay.
A little barrow painted blue,
A faithful duck on wheels for you.
Stilts to make us very tall,
Colored blocks to build a wall.

by

PAM AYRES

Illustrated by

GRAHAM PERCY

When the tree is on the ground,
All my friends will come around.
On the trunk we'll jump and climb,
We will have a lovely time!
No more tearing jacket sleeves,
No more sweeping up of leaves.
And when I'm tucked into my bed,
Kisses kissed and good-nights said,
The tree won't scare me any more,
When the night wind makes it roar.
If there wasn't any tree
What difference would it make to me?
No treehouse—that's the worst of all—
To hide in when we hear Mom call.
No cool places in the shade,
When we have run and jumped and
    played.
No leaves to kick and throw about
And roll each other in and shout.
No sticks to find on chilly days,
To make our winter fires blaze.

And there is another thing—
What will happen to our swing?
Where will owl and squirrel stay
If the tree is hauled away?
If the tree is really gone,
What can I hang my nest box on?
Suddenly we're not so sure
We want it cut down anymore.
Trees are special, large or small,
So Dad—don't cut it down *at all!*

47

An excerpt from **The Big**

Dad was so tired the next day that he didn't get up early. Mom took him a cup of tea in bed. While the rest of the family was having breakfast, they heard a loud noise in the street. They all hurried outside. A truck had arrived at their house. It was huge! It had a big drum that turned slowly round and round— CRRURK, CRRURK, CRRURK! On the side of the truck was written "JIFFY READY-MIX CONCRETE CO."

Out jumped jolly Joe Best. "Load of cement you ordered!" he called cheerfully. "Not this morning, surely?" said Mom. "I'm sure we didn't..." But it was too late. Jimmy had already pulled a lever and the big drum poured out a load of cement, all in a rush.

Slop! Slurp! Dollop! Splosh! Just like that! It landed in a shivering heap right outside the Pattersons' front door. Dad rushed downstairs, pulling on his trousers over his pajamas. "We weren't expecting you today!" he shouted. "That's o.k. Just sign here," said Joe. Then he leaped back into his seat. "It's quick-setting!" he called from the cab window. "Be hard as a rock in a couple of hours. Better get busy!" "But we haven't..." Dad called back. But Jimmy was already revving up the engine. The big cement mixer roared away up the street in a cloud of dust. "Quick!" cried Dad, picking up a shovel. "Quick!" shrieked Mom, searching for a spade.

Concrete Lorry *by Shirley Hughes*

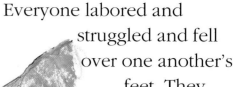

"Grab those buckets!"
"Fetch the
wheelbarrow!"
"Run for the
neighbors!"
*"The quick-
setting concrete
is soon going to set!"*
Never had the Pattersons moved so
fast. Mom began to shovel up the
concrete into the wheelbarrow and
trundle it through the house, while
Dad shoveled and smoothed it down
over the foundation in the back.
Josie and Harvey ran to fetch Mr. Lal
and Rhajit from next
door, and Frankie
and Mae's dad from
up the street.
And they all
came running.
The neighbors
pitched in and
shoveled and
spread too. Josie,
Harvey, and
little Pete ran up and down with
buckets. Murdoch joined in,
barking loudly.

Everyone labored and
struggled and fell
over one another's
feet. They
shoveled
and heaved
and trundled
concrete from the front of the house to
the back. And steadily the heap on
the pavement grew smaller
and smaller.
"Quick! It's
beginning to set!"
shouted Mom.
Everybody
worked faster
and faster.
"Done at last!"

gasped Dad, throwing down his shovel
and wiping his hands on his
trousers. Then all the
workers rested. The
foundation
was finished. Only a
small hill of concrete
was left beside the front
door. It had set so hard
that nothing in the world
would move it.

Our Dog

by Helen Oxenbury

Our dog has to go for a
walk every day. She stares
at us until we take her.

One day she found
a smelly pond and
jumped into it.

"Poo! You smell
disgusting!" we told her.
Then she rolled in the mud.
"Pretend she's not ours," whispered
Mom. "We have to get her home
quickly and give her a bath."

50

We made her wait outside
the kitchen door.
Mom filled the bathtub.
"I'll put her in," Mom said.
"Now, hold on tight! Don't let her jump out."

"Quick! Where's the towel?"
Mom shouted. "She'll get
everything wet!"

We chased her
out of the kitchen and
down the hall.

She ran up the stairs
and into the bedroom.
We caught her
on the bed.

51

"It's no use!" Mom said.
"We'll just have to take her
for another walk, to dry
in the air."

52

On Saturday night I lost my wife,
And where do you think I found her?
Up in the moon, singing a tune,
And all the stars around her.

Sally go round the sun,
Sally go round the moon,
Sally go round the chimney pots
On a Saturday afternoon.

Moon

illustrated by *Charlotte Voake*

Hey diddle, diddle,
The cat and the fiddle,
   The cow jumped over the moon.
The little dog laughed
To see such sport,
   And the dish ran away with the spoon.

The man in the moon
Came tumbling down,
   And asked his way to Norwich.
He went by the south,
And burnt his mouth
   With supping cold pease-porridge.

55

Beep beep! Here come...

THE HORRIBLES

SLOB HEAD

FAT FOOT

FRECKLE BELLY

BONE BUM

a story from *The Horribles* by

Michael Rosen

HORRIBLE BABY

illustrated by

John Watson

Horrible Baby was in its crib, gurgling. The other Horribles—Slob Head, Fat Foot, Freckle Belly, and Bone Bum—were having breakfast. They were eating dollops. There was a big pile of them in the middle of the table. Every now and then one of the Horribles grabbed a dollop and stuffed it into its mouth. But sometimes another Horrible tried to grab it first.

Fat Foot had a dollop in each hand. Slob Head grabbed one of Fat Foot's dollops, so Fat Foot wheeled around and slopped the other dollop into Slob Head's face.

This was breakfast time with the Horribles.

"I'm worried about Horrible Baby," said Slob Head. "It's not horrible enough."

"Oh, I think Horrible Baby is plenty horrible enough," said Fat Foot.

"Nonsense!" said Slob Head. "Listen to it."

The Horribles got quiet and listened.

Horrible Baby was going, "Ooofle, ooofle, ooofle!"

"Do you hear that?" said Slob Head. "It's too nice, much too nice."

Freckle Belly looked up from its dollop.

"We could teach Horrible Baby some horrible noises," said Freckle Belly.

"Yes," said Bone Bum, "like *schmarfle* and *erg durg nabber.*"

"Good," said Slob Head. "Very good."

"I'll go and get Horrible Baby," said Bone Bum.

This was Bone Bum's favorite job.

It crept very slowly up to Horrible Baby's door, then pushed the door open and roared, "GRUNKLE GRUNKLE GRUNKLE GRUNKLE GRUNKLE!!!!!!!!!!"

Horrible Baby looked at Bone Bum and smiled. "Bone Bum silly!" said Horrible Baby.

"No, Bone Bum really scary," roared Bone Bum, and then Bone Bum put its nose into its mouth, waved its arms in the air, and roared,

"UNGER UNGER UNGER UNGER UNGER UNGER!!!!!!!!"

—which was supposed to be *grunkle grunkle grunkle*, but *unger unger unger* was all Bone Bum could manage with its nose in its mouth. Horrible Baby loved it. It wasn't scared at all.

"Come on," said Bone Bum, feeling a little fed up.

"Come and have your dollops."

So Horrible Baby got up and joined the other Horribles for breakfast.

"Don't want dollops!" said Horrible Baby. "Want my bottle! Want my bottle! Want my bottle!"

"No," said Fat Foot. "You must have your dollops."

Horrible Baby started to scream. "WANT MY BOTTLE WANT MY BOTTLE WANT MY BOTTLE WANT MY BOTTLE!!!!!!!!"

Slob Head put its hands over its ears, which was very difficult because Slob Head's hands were very small and its ears were enormous.

"Oh, stop the noise! Stop the noise!" said Slob Head.

"You must have your dollops," said Fat Foot, "and then you'll grow up to be a great big Horrible."

"WANT MY 'BOTTLE WANT MY BOTTLE WANT MY BOTTLE!" Horrible Baby went on screaming.

Freckle Belly got up and put some watery mud in Horrible Baby's bottle. Horrible Baby grabbed it. Slob Head took its hands off its ears and watched. As Horrible Baby sucked on its bottle, there were long bubbly sucky noises.

Sklersh frernch! Sklersh frernch! Sklush frunch! Sklush frunch! Sklish frinch! Sklish frinch! Slob Head quickly put its hands over its ears again.

"Oh, the noise, the noise, I can't stand it!" Fat Foot said. "Listen, Horrible Baby, that's a really nasty noise, not the kind of noise we want to hear from you at all."

Freckle Belly giggled. Secretly Freckle Belly really wanted to make Horrible Baby bottle-sucking noises itself.

"It's not funny," said Slob Head. "That noise is disgusting. You could help by teaching it some regular Horrible Noises."

"All right," said Freckle Belly. "Come on, Bone Bum, come and help."

So Bone Bum and Freckle Belly took Horrible Baby into Horrible Baby's room and started to teach it Horrible Noises.

"Listen here, Horrible Baby," said Bone Bum. "When you grow up you're going to be horrible, o.k? That means when you go out, you've got to be really horrible wherever you go. You might be in the

58

street or somewhere and so you've got to learn to scream horrible noises and scare people, o.k.?"

"Like this," said Freckle Belly.

Freckle Belly lifted its arms in the air and started shaking all over. Then it roared, "Slob slob slob gluck nucker! Slob slob slob gluck nucker!"

"Now you try," said Bone Bum.

Horrible Baby looked at the two Horribles for a moment and very slowly pulled the bottle out of its mouth. There was just one more moment and then the watery mud that was supposed to be in Horrible Baby's stomach started gurgling up out of its mouth.

"Blurk blurk blurk!" said Horrible Baby, as the watery mud slithered out of its mouth and down its chin.

"Oh, no!" said Freckle Belly, turning away. "That's awful!"

"Oh, no no no no no!" said Bone Bum, and began to run away.

"Slob Head, quick, come here!" said Freckle Belly. "Horrible Baby is being terrible!"

In came Slob Head and Fat Foot.

"Now, that's really naughty," said Fat Foot. "Just look at the mess."

"I can't stand to look at it," said Freckle Belly.

"Neither can I," said Bone Bum.

"Wait a minute," said Slob Head. "I've just thought of something. Why did you go in there with Horrible Baby?"

"To teach it horrible noises, of course," said Freckle Belly.

"Well, what's the matter then?" said Slob Head.

"Well," said Bone Bum. "Horrible Baby's being naughty. It won't learn the horrible words. Instead it keeps being… er… er… er…"

"It keeps being what?" said Slob Head.

"It keeps being horrible," said Bone Bum.

"Well, all right then," said Slob Head. "Horrible Baby is being horrible."

"I don't like it," said Freckle Belly.

"I do," said Slob Head.

"Blurk blurk blurk!" said Horrible Baby.

THE YELLOW HOUSE

by
BLAKE MORRISON

illustrated by
HELEN CRAIG

Every day we passed the yellow house on our way to the park, Mom and me and my little sister Jenny. The house stood by itself. It looked old, sad, and kind of scary.

At the little wooden gate Mom would lift me up to show me the garden. There was a lawn, a goldfish pond, a greenhouse, an apple tree, a trash can, a garden gnome. But never any people, never any children.

One day Jenny dropped her teddy bear near the yellow house and Mom went back to get it. I climbed the wooden gate all by myself. In the garden was a boy wearing jeans and a hat. He waved to me.

"Come inside!" he shouted. **"Come and play with me."**

I pulled myself over and slid my legs down until they touched the pebbly path. The garden looked huge. The boy stood on the lawn.

"Come and see this!" he shouted. **"Come and see this."**

I ran and looked. In the long grass a tiger was playing with its cubs. They cuffed and scratched each other. They growled at me.

But the boy had moved off to the goldfish pond.

"Come and see this!" he shouted. **"Come and see this."**

I ran and looked. A white dolphin swam out from the lily pads, leaped in the air, and splashed down on the water. It wiggled its tail at me. But the boy had gone inside the greenhouse.

"Come and see this!" he shouted. **"Come and see this."**

60

I ran and looked. A green snake was winding its body around the stem of a tomato plant. It slithered and hissed.

It stuck out its tongue at me. But the boy was standing under the apple tree.

**"Come and see this!"
he shouted.
"Come and see this."**

I ran and looked. A pelican was roosting on a branch. It swallowed an apple with a *chomp chomp*. It wobbled its pouch at me.

But the boy had opened the trash can.

**"Come and see this!"
he shouted.
"Come and see this."**

I ran and looked. Inside the trash can a panda was reading a newspaper. It squinted and ho-hoed. It lifted its hat when it saw me.

But the boy was striding through the front door of the house.

**"Come and see this!"
he shouted.
"Come and see this."**

I ran to look but the boy had closed the door. I stretched and stretched, right up on my tiptoes, but the handle was too high for me.

I rang the bell, but no one came to answer.

Now Mom had seen me and was calling from the wooden gate. She looked angry. I walked very slowly down the pebbly path. Mom lifted me back over the gate. "Where have you been?" she asked. "Jenny was worried."

Then Mom gave me a great big kiss.

We still go past the yellow house on our way to the park, Mom and me and my little sister Jenny. Mom lifts me up to see the garden. There is a lawn, a goldfish pond, a greenhouse, an apple tree, a trash can, a garden gnome. Never any people, though, never any children, never the boy who waved to me. But I know one day he'll be there again, calling me in to play.

61

Beaky

by Jez Alborough

"I will call you Beaky. Come on, let's go for a walk."

"Am I a frog?" asked Beaky as they hopped along. Frog laughed.

"If you were a frog," he said, "then you would be able to hop as high as me and you wouldn't have those funny fluffy flaps."

"If I'm not a frog," said Beaky, "then what am I?"

"I don't know," puzzled Frog, "I've never seen anything like you before, but you must be something…everything is something!"

Before long they found Snake.

"What's he doing?" asked Beaky.

"Slithering," said Frog. "Precisely," said Snake. "It's simply splendid to slither. You should try a slither yourself."

An egg tumbled down through the leaves and branches and shattered into pieces on the rain forest floor.

Out popped a fluffy creature with a bright blue beak and a curly orange tail.

"Hello," croaked Frog, jumping out from behind a bush.

"I'm a frog, what are you?"

The creature looked confused.

"Don't you know what you are?" asked Frog.

The creature shook its head.

"Then you can be my friend," said Frog.

"Yes, try it" said Frog, for he wondered if Beaky might be some kind of snake. So Beaky lay on the earth and tried to slither. Nothing happened. "Oh dear," said Frog. Snake laughed. "Too short," he said, and slithered off into the trees. Beaky and Frog hopped to the river where they found Fish gliding in the water. "What's he doing?" asked Beaky. "I'm swimming," said Fish. "Come and join me, the water's perfect." "Good idea," said Frog, thinking that Beaky might be some kind of fish. "Try a swim." Beaky splished and splashed and flipped and flapped, but he couldn't swim a stroke. "Oh dear," said Frog. Fish giggled. "Too fluffy," he said, and swam away. "Everyone knows what they are except me," sighed Beaky. Just then he heard something singing softly, far away. "Did you hear that?" he said excitedly. "Hear what?" said Frog.

"Listen!" said Beaky. "It came from up there." Frog looked up to the top of the trees, then he heard it too. "Someone up there must be really happy," said Beaky, "to sing such a joyful song. Do you think I could ever be that happy?" "Maybe," said Frog, "but not until we discover what you are." Then he had an idea. "Let's climb up there," he said, "and see if we can find out." So up they went, but the higher they climbed the more frightened Frog became. So Beaky had to go on alone. On and on he struggled, all through the day and into the night until he could go no further.

"Now I'm lost," cried Beaky, "and I still haven't found out what I am. Maybe I should never have left the forest floor. Perhaps the song was just a dream." And with this thought, he slept.

Beaky awoke the next morning to the sound of a familiar song. Looking around, he saw a beautiful fluffy creature with a bright blue beak and a curly orange tail circling in the air.

"What are you?" called Beaky.

"I'm a bird," sang the creature. "A bird of Paradise."

"A bird," said Beaky. "That's what I am."

In his excitement he jumped and skipped and dipped, he strutted, bobbed, and trotted, and then...

he tripped!

Down and down he fell, crashing through leaves and branches, down toward the earth below.

"Flap your wings!" called the bird. "Flap your wings!"

Beaky opened wide his fluffy flaps.

"My wings," he cried, "these are my *wings*." And with a *whoosh* he began to fly... up past a tree where Snake was slithering... down to the river where Fish was swimming... and back to the vine where Frog was still waiting.

"Frog," said Beaky, "look at me. I can't slither, or swim, or hop like you, but I can *fly!*"

At that moment Beaky heard the singing once more and it seemed to be calling him.

"I must go," he said, "but I'll come back and visit."

Then he flew up toward the treetops.

"Beaky," called Frog, "you haven't told me what you are."

"I'm a bird," cried Beaky. "I'm a bird...a bird of Paradise!"

Edmond had been so excited by the sight of his new country that he had run a few steps down the other side of the hill. Now he found he could no longer see the thicket, his fields, the barn, or the farmhouse. He ran quickly to the top of the hill again and looked back the way he had come.

There was the farmhouse; he could see his bedroom window and just make out

one of his yellow curtains which had been caught by the wind and was now flapping lazily in the breeze. Edmond turned the other way and looked at his new world; he was on a boundary between the Old World and the New. He hesitated for a moment, wondering which way to go. Then his eye caught a movement quite close to him. A familiar figure was walking up the path toward him. It was his father.

Edmond gave him a half wave and turned into the New World. He walked down to the lake where the rushes grew. The ground got very boggy but there were tussocks you could stand on safely. Edmond pulled at the reeds; they were firmly rooted, but finally he got up a good long one, which he held up in front of him like a sword as he walked on around the lake.

Where the boat was moored, Edmond found that the bank was propped up by some wooden boards driven into the water. This meant you could walk right up to the edge of the lake. Lying down, he could lean over the edge, then just get his hand into the water and make some satisfactory waves that rocked the boat.

Edmond got up, pulled on the rope that moored the boat, and, when it was against the bank, jumped in. In the boat were oars, but they were too big for Edmond to use, although he

FAR AWAY

by Martin Bax
illustrated by Michael Foreman

could just lift them. Just then Edmond's father came up. He put down a big bundle he was carrying, untied the rope that moored the boat and, stepping down into it, pushed them out into the lake. Edmond was surprised to see how well his father rowed. They rowed out to the center of the lake because Edmond wanted to speak to the swan. But the swan swam away from them in a circle. They rowed after it, but it kept circling. They tried to row straight toward it. It looked at them, but it bowed its head twice at them, very politely, and then swam away.

They moored the boat again and Edmond walked around the lake, picking up wood that had collected at the edge. In his bundle, Edmond's father had a frying pan and some sausage. They built a fire with the driftwood and ate sausage and baked beans, and filled up with bags of potato chips.

By now it was quite dark

and the moon had come up. Edmond was glad to find that his father had brought him his sleeping bag. They had built their fire a little up the hill from the lake. Edmond could snuggle down and look out over the water. Wreaths of mist spiraled up from the

lake. They looked, Edmond thought, like ghostly people, but friendly because they came from his lake. As they grew bigger he saw that they had the faces of all the people he liked best, all the people he had left at home when he had come far away.

NONSENSE RHYMES

Gregory Griggs,
Gregory Griggs,
Had twenty-seven different wigs.
He wore them up,
He wore them down,
To please the people of the town;
He wore them east,
He wore them west;
But he never could tell
Which he liked best.

Old Mother Shuttle
Lived in a coal scuttle,
Along with her dog and her cat;
What they ate I can't tell,
But 'tis known very well,
That not one of the party was fat.

Old Mother Shuttle
Scoured out her coal scuttle,
And washed both her dog and her cat;
The cat scratched her nose,
So they came to hard blows
And who was the gainer by that?

illustrated by Nicola Bayley

I dreamed a dream next Tuesday week,
Beneath the apple trees;
I thought my eyes were big pork pies,
And my nose was Stilton cheese.
The clock struck twenty minutes to six,
When a frog sat on my knee;
I asked him to lend me eighteen pence,
But he borrowed a shilling of me.

There was an old lady of Wales,
Who lived upon oysters and snails.
Upon growing a shell,
She exclaimed, "It is well,
I won't have to wear bonnets or veils."

MRS. GOOSE'S

One day Mrs. Goose found an egg and made a lovely nest to put it in. Mrs. Goose sat on the egg to keep it safe and warm.

Soon the egg started to crack open. The little bird inside was pecking at the shell.

Mrs. Goose's baby was very very small and fluffy and yellow.

Mrs. Goose took her baby out to eat some grass. But her baby didn't want to eat grass. She ran off to look for something different.

Mrs. Goose took her naughty baby to the pond. The water looked cold and gray. Poor Mrs. Goose! Her baby would not swim!

BABY

by Charlotte Voake

The baby grew and grew and grew.

Mrs. Goose's feathers were smooth and white.

Mrs. Goose's baby had untidy brown feathers.

Mrs. Goose had large webbed feet.

Her baby had little pointed toes.

The baby followed Mrs. Goose everywhere

and cuddled up to her at night.

Mrs. Goose guarded her baby from strangers.

Mrs. Goose's baby never did eat much grass.

The baby never did go swimming in the pond.

And everyone except Mrs. Goose knew why.

Mrs. Goose's baby was a CHICKEN!

A House in Town

by William Mayne
illustrated by
Sarah Fox-Davies

Foxy mother Vixen lives in the town. One night she stalks her prey along the hills high above the houses.

Another night she forages from bins and heaps beside the shops and houses of the town.

This night she crossed the river to hunt in woods still wild.

"I see her late at night and early in the day," the bridge-keeper tells his friends. "She does not need to pay to pass."

This night is turning into day when Vixen comes to her children hidden in the town, beneath a house in a sloping street: Rack, and Rennie, and little Ryll. By day they sleep. By night they watch the door and wait. In and out come shadows—Fox, their father, Vixen mother.

The night is turning into day when she rounds without a sound the last street corner.

There, instead of empty street and stillness, is a gang of men. Vixen crouches on a wall to see and hear. The men are at her house with large machines like birds, tall and beaked, pecking, eating, at her home.

Vixen listens for her husband, Fox. She hears machines; she smells falling dust; she sees breaking house; she feels awful fear.

She runs under wheels, among feet, between falling stones. She creeps to the door and jumps. No man sees her.

Rack and Rennie and little Ryll are already wakened, terrified. There is no sign of Fox, their father, who is hunting far and wide tonight.

Vixen has to do the best she can alone. She knows what it must be. Little Ryll she carries, because she cannot walk. Rack and Rennie follow.

"Stay close," says Vixen. "We'll run like one; they will not see us pass."

They come into the gardens of a city square. Rack and Rennie love the day and want to run about. Little Ryll has tried and cannot tumble very far.

"We must go," says Vixen. She sees an empty street. It leads upward, a weary way to the hills and another home.

That street, and yet another street, they walk. Their tongues hang out. They creep from gate to gate; they crawl from tree to tree; they slink through garden hedge and fence.

Rack grows tired; Rennie lags behind. Vixen goes ahead.

In front of Rack and Rennie walks a terrier dog. He does not see them, though they see him and know of danger in their hearts. He sees Vixen with little Ryll.

His hackles rise. He calls out. He knows that Vixen is a fox. He calls again for other dogs to help, and begins the hunt. He has dreamed of chase and this is it.

Vixen looks back for Rack and Rennie. They are not close. All she can do is run.

Rack and Rennie look at each other, frightened now. They lie low and wait. What to do they cannot tell: they have not learned to live or stay alive.

Vixen goes on up the hill. Toward her run two spotted dogs. From an alley runs a fattish beagle out of breath, and its master just the same.

Vixen cannot go on up the hill. She turns aside. She knows all the city ways. A playful puppy thinks it will win at once and tips Vixen over in the road.

Vixen drops poor Ryll and bites the pup. But spotted dogs are upon her, beagle, terrier, and more. When they've gone, and Vixen too, Ryll is sitting all alone and whimpering.

73

Rack and Rennie run to her. Rack picks her up. Rennie sniffs the ground. "This way," she says, and sets off down the hill, where Vixen went before.

They follow on. Where Vixen ran the scent is clear for them. It is clear too for dogs, and they begin to come behind. The way is very hard, where Vixen scrambled up a wall, along the top, and down a dizzy gate; or squeezed through a narrow drain. Dogs come out of all the houses.

Rack has to stop. He has no breath. He puts Ryll down and Rennie carries her. They run on again, but very slow, though down the hill.

A strange thing happens now behind them. The chasing dogs run off to the right, along a different street. The reason is soon clear. Padding fast and gentle there comes Fox, their father. "Go on," he says, "your mother's making for the bridge. I'll cross your track and cross your trail, and draw the pack away. But hurry on and do not wait for me," he calls, and swiftly goes.

Hurry on they do, by factories and railways, where Vixen's scent is leading them.

All the time the dogs are calling in the streets behind. Ahead of Rack and Rennie sirens sound where police cars clear the road for them. Foxes cannot know of that, or how men come on the street to see them pass by day. The little foxes only know that they must run.

At a crossroads all the traffic lights are red. In the middle Vixen waits, not knowing if the cubs are safe.

Rennie drops young Ryll. Vixen gives all three a lick, tells them they must hurry yet, and leads the way. The traffic waits and watches. It seems that men can do no more to help, nor stop the pack of dogs.

The dogs run wildly down the hill, all noise. In front, and turning now and then to tease, is Fox, loping just ahead.

Vixen is on the bridge. The wild woods lie beyond. Out of breath beside her, Rack and Rennie walk. In her jaws is Ryll. No man or truck, car or bus, is with them now.

They cross the river. Men begin to clap their hands, pleased at the escape.

"It does not help," says Vixen. "We are not safe. Dogs are coming too." She looks back. But when she does she sees a gap begin to open in the road, where the keeper lifts the bridge so no dog can cross that place. He does not know that Fox is still to follow.

The dogs come on and on. Fox is tired now, his ears more flat. Vixen's heart stands still in pain; men clap their hands no more:

they did not know of Fox and see no escape for him. Fox runs on the bridge, up the lifting road to the gap, and looks at it. He sits there calm. The dogs run up to him, and when they do he rises to his toes and jumps, clear across the gap and to the other side. "Good day, gentlemen," he says to them, and turns away to smile at Vixen and the cubs.

Crawling, yelping dogs fall off the bridge, through the gap and into water, over the edge and into mud. Some swim up the docks, others muddle back to land; none cross the river.

Now that Fox is safe, men clap again and cheer. Vixen's heart begins to beat once more.

Fox licks her nose for love. The family, together now and safe, hurry under the trees.

The keeper of the bridge has his picture in the paper for kindness to creatures of the woods still wild.

Judy the Bad Fairy

by *Martin Waddell*
illustrated by
Dom Mansell

The Fairy Queen had a Good Long Think, and then she snapped her fingers and said, " T E E T H ! "

"Teeth?" said Judy, halfway to her hammock. "I'm putting you on teeth!" the Fairy Queen snapped. "You can be Tooth Fairy for the Realm. Here's your Tooth Bag, and here's your Under-the-Pillow Money. Bring back at least fourteen teeth each night at midnight, OR ELSE!"

Fourteen teeth is a lot of teeth. Poor Judy had to move fast. Most of the poor people had either no teeth or very black ones, so by and large she stuck to the castle. Most of the people in the castle had bedrooms at the top of the tall towers. Upstairs and downstairs ran Judy at top speed, teeth-gathering and money-under-pillow-dumping.

"I've fixed her this time!" said the Fairy Queen delightedly. And all the Good Fairies held a Fairy Party to celebrate, and took turns lying in Judy's honeysuckle hammock.

Judy got so tired that her Fairy Legs wouldn't work any more. She sank down halfway up the tallest tower, and lay there like a dead Fairy. Then...

PUFF!
Pant!
Phew!

SNORE! SNORE! SNORE! SNORE!

The snoring was coming from behind a door. Judy opened it, looking for a place to lie down. And…it was the King's Auntie Chamber! All the King's Aunties were asleep there.

Each one had a little bed all to herself, and beside each little bed there was a little table, and on each little table there was a little glass, and in each little glass there was …a set of T E E T H !
Judy grabbed the nearest glass.
There were twenty-eight teeth in it, which meant Judy was able to take the weekend off in the honeysuckle hammock, and still hand in fourteen teeth each night at the stroke of twelve.

Eat Up, Gemma

by Sarah Hayes
illustrated by
Jan Ormerod

One morning we woke up late. I couldn't find my shoes and Gemma wouldn't eat her breakfast. "Eat up, Gemma," said Mom, but Gemma threw her breakfast on the floor. Later on we went to the market. Mom bought a bag of apples and some bananas. The man at the fruit stall gave me a bunch of grapes. He gave some to Gemma too. "Eat up, Gemma," said the man, but Gemma pulled the grapes off one by one and squashed them.

When we got home Grandma had made the dinner. "Nice and spicy," Dad said, "just how I like it." It was nice and spicy all right. I drank three glasses of water. "Eat up, Gemma," said Grandma. Gemma banged her spoon on the table and shouted. But she didn't eat a thing. The next day was Saturday and Dad took us to the park. We had chocolate cookies for a treat. I ate two and then another two. "Eat up, Gemma," said Dad. But Gemma didn't eat her cookie. She just licked off all the chocolate and gave the rest to the birds.

In the evening our friends were having a party. "Eat up, everyone," said our friends. And we did, all except Gemma. She sat on Grandma's knee and gave her dinner to the dog when Grandma wasn't looking.

After the party my friend came to stay and we had a midnight feast. Gemma didn't have any. She was too tired. In the morning we made Gemma a feast. "Eat up, Gemma," said my friend. Gemma picked up her toy hammer and banged her feast to pieces. My friend thought it was funny, but Mom and Dad didn't.

Soon it was time for us to put on our best clothes and go to church. I sang very loudly. The lady in front of us had a hat with fruit on it. I could see Gemma looking and looking.

When everyone was really quiet Gemma leaned forward. "Eat up, Gemma," she said.

Then she tried to pull a grape off the lady's hat. She pulled and pulled and the lady's hat fell off. Gemma hid her face in Dad's coat.

"Eat up, Gemma," I said. And she did. She ate all the grapes and the bananas. She even tried to eat the skins.

"Thank goodness for that," said Mom.

"We were getting worried," said Dad.

Grandma smiled at me. I felt very proud.

"Gemma eat up," said Gemma, and we all laughed.

When we got home I had an idea. I found a plate and a bowl. I turned the bowl upside down and put it on the plate. Then I took a bunch of grapes and two bananas and put them on the plate. It looked just like the lady's hat.

LITTLE RABBIT FOO FOO

retold by
Michael Rosen

illustrated by
Arthur Robins

Little Rabbit Foo Foo riding through the forest, scooping up the field mice and bopping them on the head.

Down came the Good Fairy and said, "Little Rabbit Foo Foo, I don't like your attitude, scooping up the field mice and bopping them on the head. I'm going to give you three chances to change, and if you don't, I'm going to turn you into a **goonie**."

Little Rabbit Foo Foo riding through the forest, scooping up the wriggly worms and bopping them on the head.

Down came the Good Fairy and said, "Little Rabbit Foo Foo, I don't like your attitude, scooping up the wriggly worms and bopping them on the head. You've got two chances to change, and if you don't, I'm going to turn you into a **goonie**."

Little Rabbit Foo Foo riding through the forest, scooping up the tigers and bopping them on the head.

Down came the Good Fairy and said, "Little Rabbit Foo Foo, I don't like your attitude, scooping up the tigers and bopping them on the head. You've got one chance left to change, and if you don't, I'm going to turn you into a **goonie**."

Little Rabbit Foo Foo riding through the forest, scooping up the goblins and bopping them on the head.

Down came the Good Fairy and said, "Little Rabbit Foo Foo, I don't like your attitude, scooping up the goblins and bopping them on the head. "You've got no chances left, so I'm going to turn you into a **goonie**."

Sally and the Limpet

by Simon James

Not long ago, on a Sunday, Sally was down at the beach exploring, when she found a brightly colored, bigger-than-usual limpet shell. She wanted to take it home but, as she pulled, the limpet made a little squelching noise and held on to the rock. The harder Sally tugged, the more tightly the limpet held on, until, suddenly, Sally slipped and fell— with the limpet stuck to her finger.

Though she pulled with all her might, it just wouldn't come off. So she ran over to her dad. He heaved and groaned, but the limpet made a little squelching noise and held on even tighter.

So, that afternoon, Sally went home in the car with a limpet stuck to her finger. When they got home, her dad tried using his tools.

Her brother tried offering it lettuce and a cucumber.

But, that night, Sally went to bed with a limpet stuck to her finger.

Next day it was school. All her friends tried to pull the limpet off her finger.

Mr. Wobblyman, the nature teacher, said that limpets live for twenty years, and stay all their lives on the same rock.

In the afternoon, Sally's mother took her to the hospital to see the doctor. He tried chemicals, injections, potions, and pinchers.

Sally was beginning to feel upset. Everyone was making too much fuss all around her. She kicked over the doctor's chair and ran. She ran through the endless corridors. She just wanted to be on her own. She ran out of the hospital and through the town. She didn't stop when she got to the beach. She ran through people's sand castles. She even ran over a fat man.

When she reached the water, she jumped in with all her clothes on. Sally landed with a big splash and then just sat in the water.

The limpet, feeling at home once more, made a little squelching noise and wiggled off her finger.

But Sally didn't forget what Mr. Wobblyman, the nature teacher, had said. Very carefully, she lifted the limpet by the top of its shell. She carried it back across the beach, past the fat man she had walked on, and gently, so gently, she put the limpet back on the very same rock where she had found it the day before.

Then, humming to herself, she took the long way home across the beach.

an excerpt from Pog

Pog painted

by Peter Haswell

Pog painted the ceiling red.

He painted the wall red.

He painted the floor red.

He painted the fireplace red.

Pog painted the chair red.

He painted his boots red.

He painted his feet red.

Pog said, "I don't know

why I did all that ...

I
don't
really like
red!"

The Grumpalump

by Sarah Hayes
illustrated by Barbara Firth

The bear stared at
the grumpalump.
The lump grumped.

The bear stared and the
cat sat on the grumpalump.
The lump grumped.

The bear stared, the cat sat,
and the mole rolled
   on the grumpalump.
      The lump grumped.

The bear stared, the cat sat,
the mole rolled, and the dove
shoved the grumpalump.
The lump still grumped.

The bear stared, the cat sat,
the mole rolled, the dove
shoved, and the bull
pulled the grumpalump.
The lump still grumped.

The bear stared,
the cat sat, the mole
rolled, the dove shoved,
the bull pulled, and the yak whacked
the grumpalump.
The lump still grumped.

The bear stared, the cat sat,
the mole rolled, the dove shoved,
the bull pulled, the yak whacked,
and the armadillo
used it for a pillow.
But the lump still
grumped.

Then the
gnu blew.

The lump grew plump, and got
humps and bumps, bits and bobs
and interesting knobs,
and wings and things
attached with strings.
And still the
gnu blew.

Then, to everyone's surprise,
the grumpalump began to rise.
The gnu drew breath and clambered in.
The grumpalump began to grin.
"I'm off on a trip in my hot air ship,"
said the gnu, and flew.
Absolutely true.

And how the bear stared.

Hello, Goodbye

A tree stood quietly
in the sunshine.
A big brown bear
stepped up.
"Hello!" he said,
very loudly.

Hello!

Two bees flew over.
"Hello! Hello!"
they said, very busily.
Along came a big
red bird.
What did the bird say?
"Hello!"—very quickly.
Soon voices all over the
tree were saying, "Hello!"
Little voices on the leaves
said, "Hello!"
Squeaky voices on the
branches said, "Hello!"
Deep-down voices among
the roots said, "Hello!"

hello!

Hello!

by David Lloyd
illustrated by Louise Voce

Goodbye!

Suddenly a drop of rain
fell on the bear's nose.
Splash!
Raindrops fell all
over the bear.
Splash! Splash! Splash!
"Goodbye! Goodbye!"
said the two bees,
very busily.
"Goodbye!" said the big
red bird, very quickly.
What did all the voices
on the tree say? "Goodbye!"
What did the bear say,
very loudly?
"Goodbye!"
Everyone had gone.
The tree stood
quietly again.
"Hello, rain!" it said,
very, very quietly.

93